Acting Edition

Theater Masters' Take Ten Volume VII

Doormat
by Justine Gelfman

Gold Gone Right
by Rudi Goblen

The Only Thing You Came to Hear
by Thaddeus McCants

The Idiots
by Prashant Nashi

(Un)Scripted
by Dave Osmundsen

blooms
by a.k. payne

**Sahi Vaqt Pe *or* The One
with the Biological Clock**
by Ankita Raturi

Every Man's Memorial Marked
by Maria D. Smith

FOR PRODUCTION INQUIRIES
UNITED STATES AND CANADA
info@concordtheatricals.com
1-866-979-0447
UNITED KINGDOM AND EUROPE
licensing@concordtheatricals.co.uk
020-7054-7298

Each title is subject to availability from Concord Theatricals Corp., depending upon country of performance. Please be aware that *THEATER MASTERS' TAKE TEN VOLUME VII* may not be licensed by Concord Theatricals Corp. in your territory. Professional and amateur producers should contact the nearest Concord Theatricals Corp. office or licensing partner to verify availability.

advised to apply to the appropriate agent before starting rehearsals, advertising, or booking a theatre. A licensing fee must be paid whether the title(s) is presented for charity or gain and whether or not admission is charged. Professional/Stock licensing fees are quoted upon application to Concord Theatricals Corp.

This work is published by Samuel French, an imprint of Concord Theatricals Corp.

No one shall make any changes in this title(s) for the purpose of production. No part of this book may be reproduced, stored in a retrieval system, scanned, uploaded, or transmitted in any form, by any means, now known or yet to be invented, including mechanical, electronic, digital, photocopying, recording, videotaping, or otherwise, without the prior written permission of the publisher. No one shall share this title(s), or any part of this title(s), through any social media or file hosting websites.

For all inquiries regarding motion picture, television, online/digital and other media rights, please contact Concord Theatricals Corp.

MUSIC AND THIRD-PARTY MATERIALS USE NOTE

Licensees are solely responsible for obtaining formal written permission from copyright owners to use copyrighted music and/or other copyrighted third-party materials (e.g., artworks, logos) in the performance of this play and are strongly cautioned to do so. If no such permission is obtained by the licensee, then the licensee must use only original music and materials that the licensee owns and controls. Licensees are solely responsible and liable for clearances of all third-party copyrighted materials, including without limitation music, and shall indemnify the copyright owners of the play(s) and their licensing agent, Concord Theatricals Corp., against any costs, expenses, losses and liabilities arising from the use of such copyrighted third-party materials by licensees. For music, please contact the appropriate music licensing authority in your territory for the rights to any incidental music.

IMPORTANT BILLING AND CREDIT REQUIREMENTS

If you have obtained performance rights to this title, please refer to your licensing agreement for important billing and credit requirements.

THEATER MASTERS STAFF / BOARD

Victoria Hansen, Artistic Director
Emily Zemba, Associate Artistic Director
Lulu Guzman, Artistic Administrator
Julia Hansen, Founder & Artistic Advisor

Advisory Board: Chris Ashley, Alec Baldwin, Andre Bishop, Scott Ellis, Doug Hughes, Judy Kaye, Andrew Leynse, John Lithgow, Robert Moss, Brian Murray, Jack O'Brien, Neil Pepe, Theresa Rebeck, John Rando, Tim Sanford, A.R. Gurney (emeritus, 1930-2017), Gordon Davidson (emeritus, 1933-2016)

Board of Directors: Leyla Bader, Susan Buckley, Danielle Chock, Julia Hansen, Victoria Hansen, Gerri Karetsky, Marianne Lubar, Amy Rose Marsh, Naomi McDougall Jones, Sofia Milonas, Virginia Pearce, Jessica Salet, Nancy Stevens, Charlotte Tripplehorn, Daisy Walker

THEATER MASTERS 2021 STAFF

Daisy Walker, Executive Artistic Director
Victoria Hansen, Co-Artistic Director
Emily Dzioba, Artistic Administrator
Julia Hansen, Founder & Artistic Advisor

NATIONAL ADJUDICATOR 2021

James Anthony Tyler

TAKE TEN 2021 PRODUCTION STAFF

Kelly Martindale, Stage Manager
Stephen Cedars, Sound Designer
Judy Bowman CSA, Casting
Amberrain Andrews, Assistant to Dennis A. Allen II
Ana Radulescu, Assistant to Sanaz Ghajar
Elizabeth Emanuel, Closed Captioning for *Sahi Vaqt Pe*
Pauline Hilborn, Graphic Design

INTRODUCTION

Julia Hansen founded the National MFA Playwrights Competition and the TAKE TEN Festival in 2007 when she saw the need to bridge the gap between the academic training playwrights were receiving and the professional careers that lay ahead of them.

TAKE TEN's professional development opportunities and partnership with Concord Theatricals provide playwrights with a career-igniting entrance into the entertainment industry and introduce their work to the American theatre.

Each year, we invite MFA playwrights from some of the top dramatic writing programs in the country to submit a ten-minute play. In the spring, the six-to-ten winning playwrights are flown to New York for an Equity showcase production of their plays featuring professional directors and actors. Due to the ongoing Covid-19 pandemic, we kept this experience virtual as we did in 2020, giving these talented students a meaningful and substantial experience online. We consider ourselves lucky to continue to guide these young playwrights into the industry and provide a platform for their exploration of the American theatre.

This year's festival of produced Zoom readings involved talented actors, directors, and industry professionals from around the country. Our winning playwrights were mentored by James Anthony Tyler, who gave them generous feedback and insight as a working playwright. We are proud that their plays are living beyond their virtual life and are being published by Concord Theatricals.

We are grateful to all who have supported our 2021 National MFA Playwrights Festival: the MFA programs across the country, including Arizona State University, Brown University, Carnegie Mellon University, Northwestern University, New York University, University of Iowa, University of Texas at Austin, University of California Los Angeles, University of California San Diego, and the David Geffen School of Drama at Yale University, who recognize talented students; our directors Dennis A. Allen II and Sanaz Ghajar, who shared their time, expertise, and vision with our artists; our actors from far and wide who lent their talents; and finally, our generous individual donors and Board of Directors who make TAKE TEN possible.

We are passionate about these playwrights, and we hope you will enjoy this newest anthology of Theater Masters' plays.

Sincerely,
Daisy Walker, *Executive Artistic Director*
and Vicky Hansen, *Co-Artistic Director (2021)*

TABLE OF CONTENTS

Doormat

Justine Gelfman

DOORMAT was first produced by Theater Masters via Zoom on May 19, 2021. The performance was directed by Sanaz Ghajar. The production stage manager was Kelly Martindale. The cast was as follows:

JENNY . . . . Kimberly Chatterjee
SARAH . . . . Kristin Villanueva
BOSS . . . . .Andrea Syglowski

CHARACTERS

JENNY – the new assistant, female-identifying
SARAH – the old assistant, female-identifying
BOSS – the boss, female-identifying

TIME

now-ish

(Corporate heaven.)

("The Boss" by Diana Ross plays*.)

*(**JENNY** is new.)*

BOSS. jenny, welcome!

this is sarah, my old assistant

she'll be training you before she leaves

*(**SARAH** is a doormat.)*

JENNY. this is your?

BOSS. assistant, sarah

my old assistant

well, former

or current

right now, but she'll be gone soon

sarah, say hi!

(Beat.)

she likes your skirt.

JENNY. oh uh thanks!

wait –

---

* A license to produce *Doormat* does not include a performance license for "The Boss." The publisher and author suggest that the licensee contact ASCAP or BMI to ascertain the music publisher and contact such music publisher to license or acquire permission for performance of the song. If a license or permission is unattainable for "The Boss," the licensee may not use the song in *Doormat* but should create an original composition in a similar style or use a similar song in the public domain. For further information, please see the Music and Third Party Materials Use Note on page iii.

    i'm just confused
    this is sarah?

BOSS. yes!

JENNY. oh okay
    cool
    (To **SARAH.***)* hi!

BOSS. she's eating,
    so we'll let her finish lunch

        (They walk.)

    i love her,
    but i can't eat a salad every day
    i don't know how she does it
    bird food
    but that's sarah
    she's sweet and simple
    and has been really quiet since last month
    bob, our CEO
    had a holiday party for all of us
    and when he talked to sarah
    he was uh,
    what's the word?
    really inappropriate and drunk
    and look –
    he's had a hard year,
    i'll give him that
    his wife had breast cancer
    and she's totally fine now
    they caught it super early,
    but still, you know uh
    tough

JENNY. wow

    i'm glad she's ok

BOSS. me too, i love his wife

    it's weird though,

    sarah's been like that ever since,

    subdued, not taking charge

    i always thought

    she'd stay in this navy rolly chair

    for five years

    and we'd have some inside jokes

    and i'd give her half my clementine

    that my husband packs for me

    we're religious about meal prep

    and eventually i'd write her a letter of rec

    that i'd feel conflicted about

    because i don't really want her to leave,

    but i also want to support her

    but i guess, it's time to move on

JENNY. oh i'm sorry

    that sucks

BOSS. no, it's totally fine!

    i was just emotionally unprepared

    when she put in her two weeks

    two weeks ago

    it was so out of the blue,

    but i'm happy that this worked out

    and you can come in

    and train with her

    i think it's gonna be a great fit!

JENNY. yeah, definitely

i loved talking with you

this is exactly what i'm looking for

BOSS. yay!

me too!

JENNY. yay!

me too

BOSS. me too

JENNY. me too

BOSS. me too

JENNY. me too

BOSS. me too

(Beat.)

do you ever say a word so much

that it loses its meaning

and becomes just tasteless and blurry,

like rice pudding?

JENNY. sure

BOSS. it's so strange, jenny

you remind me of sarah

but also, not at all

JENNY. oh uh, thank you?

BOSS. so after you finish

training with her,

i'll come get you

and we can go over any questions

also – no pressure at all,

but if you do a little digging,

find out what she's doing next

JENNY. oh, sure!

i'll do my best

BOSS. because just between us,

i'm so curious

i heard a rumor

that she's moving into her mom's basement

or that she got a job with healthcare

but that probably isn't true

people love to gossip here

so be careful with your secrets

last month, sharon at reception spilled the beans

about mike in accounting's affair

with elaine in development

and let me tell you: it was not pretty

fuck sharon, but also, go sharon!

so honestly, who knows with sarah

i love her,

but it's not my problem,

but i'd love to make it my problem

see, that's a pattern i do

i figured that out with my therapist last week

i have a problem of

taking on other people's problems,

so i'm trying to work through that

and while i think it's selfless,

my therapist said it's actually selfish

so i'm trying to be a little more selfish

JENNY. oh

nice

i love therapy

BOSS. ME TOO!

JENNY. yeah, it's great

it should be free

BOSS. agreed!

jenny!

this is going to work out well

it's funny though

well – don't judge me

but i used to find sarah sort of annoying

in the mornings,

she would come into the office and *smile*

and take off her coat and *smile*

and go to the keurig and *smile*

and i was like:

who the fuck do you think you are?

a fucking robot, like siri or alexa

all those robots are named after women

which is another thing i figured out in therapy

but women in the workplace

we fought to not smile

so just, like: simmer, sarah

but now, she's sort of *flat*

it's weird

she interviewed really well here

better than you, honestly

she remembered little things about my life

about my family and my schedule

and never asked me how to do stuff

she just googled it, but silently

it was amazing

she was amazing at google

maybe she *was* siri
but now, she just sits there
and i don't know
i feel bad
she's like a breadstick
she seems lonely

JENNY. yeah, that is sad

    (Beat.)

did you ever talk to her about it?

BOSS. no, no, no, *no*
i feel like that's inappropriate
and these things happen all the time
with work relationships
we live and we learn
or we don't live and we don't learn
and we have
SO MUCH WORK TO DO
and if we repeat our mistakes,
so be it, you know?
wait, do you know *wiggle*?
that's our operating system
it's fucking terrible
i hate it
it's weird having a system that sucks
and really is good for no one
but we just keep using it
we just keep using the bad operating system
and when we acquire companies
or onboard people

we just keep using the bad systems
because it would be too much work
to change
to not use *wiggle*, i mean
i don't even know what the office
would look like without it
we'd probably fold
or get sold
or i'd have to bleach my hair blonde
and shave it all off,
don't you think?

JENNY. or maybe it's possible to –

BOSS. so sarah can show you,
how to use *wiggle*
i remember when i first learned it
it made me want to unzip my skin
and crawl out of it,
like a tent in the pacific northwest
that you share with a boy
who went to oberlin
that you're somehow dating,
which reminds me: are you dating anyone?

JENNY. no, i'm not
not at the moment
no
nope

BOSS. good, good
i like to use metaphors
i like incorporating creative solutions
into my work
except no one is receptive to my solutions

JENNY. well, i'm sure that's not true

BOSS. no, it is!
    basically when i first got hired
    i figured out no one listened to me
    i was really good at being wallpaper
    and writing things down
    which some men see and think:
    secretary
    but i saw and thought:
    nancy drew
    so i acted like nancy drew
    and just inhaled company culture
    i kept copious notes
    and descriptions and details
    all the snarky comments
    the inappropriate advances
    the mean take downs
    i filed them all away
    and then, i got a promotion,
    which was awesome!
    so i decided to burn my files
    to make space for
    my new company computer
    they gave me a computer!
    and if i focused on my computer,
    i could sometimes
    help my friends or assistants
    excuse me, colleagues!
    i love that word
    no idea what it means,
    but it feels athletic, right?

so seriously,

you can come to me with anything

because *i get it*

    (Back at the desk.)

    (SARAH *is a real person.)*

SARAH. hey jenny!

i pulled over a rolly chair for you

JENNY. oh, hi!

SARAH. let me just throw out my salad,

one sec –

    (SARAH *tosses her salad.)*

BOSS. don't have too much fun

i'll leave you two to it

    (BOSS *exits.)*

JENNY. uh sorry, who are you?

SARAH. sarah

    (Beat.)

JENNY. *oh*

oh fuck, i'm so sorry about that,

i didn't realize –

SARAH. no, it's fine

everyone thinks i'm a victim here

but i'm not

    (Beat.)

JENNY. right

well

it's nice to meet you

SARAH. you too
and i wasn't kidding
i actually like your skirt

JENNY. oh, thanks

SARAH. don't worry,
you'll be fine here though

JENNY. will i?

SARAH. yeah
i think so
sure

JENNY. is that why you're leaving?

SARAH. no
i uh
just got tired

JENNY. of the same job?

SARAH. eh
more of the people
wiping their shit on me

JENNY. huh, right

(*Beat.*)

well, thanks
by the way

SARAH. for what?

JENNY. for sticking around
training me

SARAH. oh yeah, of course

JENNY. so *wiggle*?

SARAH. ugh, it's awful

JENNY. i heard

SARAH. but i have
     some tricks of the trade
     passed down before my time
     i can show you

JENNY. that would be great

SARAH. also, let me give you my number
     you can text me
     if you ever have any questions

JENNY. wait, seriously?

SARAH. yeah i mean
     i know that's like illegal here
     but sometimes
     it's nice to just have a sounding board

          (SARAH *smiles.*)

          (JENNY *does too.*)

JENNY. that would be awesome

SARAH. i wish i had that
     but i guess there's always google

JENNY. yeah, google is amazing

SARAH. actually, i got this doormat
     from a google search
     off etsy,
     it was five dollars

JENNY. no way

SARAH. yeah, i think i remember where
     let me look
     do you use a doormat?

JENNY. not really

SARAH. ok, well it rains a lot here
    your feet can get kind of dirty
    a lot of mud
    coming in and out
    i didn't use one at first
    but i think,
    it's just a good thing to have

End of Play

Gold Gone Right

By Rudi Goblen

THE SHRINE: GOLD GONE RIGHT was first produced by Theater Masters via Zoom on May 20, 2021. The performance was directed by Dennis A. Allen II. The production stage manager was Kelly Martindale. The cast was as follows:

FELO. . . . . Eden Marryshow

COOTI . . . . .Lynnette R. Freeman

KAREN GOLD. . . . . Betsy Hogg

THE JUDGE. . . . . Harmonica Sunbeam

CHARACTERS

FELO – man.

> black or non-white passing latinx.

> a ceramicist.

> cooti's husband.

COOTI – woman.

> black or non-white passing latinx.

> a tomato cropper.

> felo's wife.

KAREN GOLD – a beautiful, white, blonde woman of whatever age – so damn beautiful she's ugly. if she's old, she'll look like dolly parton. if she's young, she'll look like elle woods.

THE JUDGE – a black or non-white passing latinx drag queen in a beautiful gown – aka a judge's robe, but make it fashion. she's fine and fierce; good-humored and ill-tempered. think rupaul and judge judy's baby.

SETTING

the shrine.

TIME

always.

SCRIPT NOTES

(beat) = a quick breath

(rest) = a longer breath

italicized text = emphasis on a word

(silence) = a moment to think/let things settle

— = a change of thought or an actor being cut off by another

(beats, rests, and silences should all be treated as musical notations to honor the pace of the language)

ONE

("good morning" by kanye west plays*)

*(**COOTI** enters a loft cottage in the surroundings of somewhere in the shrine. she's carrying a basket of the most delicious tomatoes)*

(she is happy—truly)

(safe and humming)

(she places the tomatoes down)

(she lowers the music)

*(**FELO** is still in bed. she wakes him up)*

COOTI. *(portuguese)* Bon diiiiaaaaaaaa.

FELO. *(waking up)* My love.

*(**COOTI** shuts the music off)*

COOTI. You ready to keep manifesting god on earth?

FELO. *(eyes still closed)* Was James Brown?

---

* A license to produce *Gold Gone Right* does not include a performance license for "Good Morning." The publisher and author suggest that the licensee contact ASCAP or BMI to ascertain the music publisher and contact such music publisher to license or acquire permission for performance of the song. If a license or permission is unattainable for "Good Morning," the licensee may not use the song in *Gold Gone Right* but should create an original composition in a similar style or use a similar song in the public domain. For further information, please see the Music and Third Party Materials Use Note on page iii.

COOTI. Haa.

FELO. *(waking up/spanish)* Por supuesto que si. Ain't that why we was put on earth for?

COOTI. Your mouth to God's ears, baby.

FELO. How long was I out?

COOTI. Not long at all.

Bout thirty-two hours and twelve minutes.

FELO. Hm, a cat nap.

I'm just so excited to make these new pinch pots.

> (**FELO** *hops out of the bed and walks towards his pottery wheel*)

> (*surrounding it is his new collection of pinch pots. some painted and finished, others still drying and grey*)

COOTI. *(sorting her tomatoes)* The now is yours.

FELO. The now is *ours*.

COOTI. *(smiles)*

FELO. How your tomatoes looking?

COOTI. *(spanish)* Ricisimo—como tu.

FELO. *(smiles) How* did I get so lucky to have married the *best-ess*, cunning cropper on all sides of the river?

To carry your last name behind my first is a trophy,

a pyramid as a gift made of a million smiling hearts.

A hug from the sun. My feet in warm, black and brown sand. The first bite of a pitted date.

COOTI. Boy, stop.

FELO. *(going back to sleep)* Okay.

COOTI. No!

> *(beat)*

Keep going.

FELO. *(turning back around)* You

are *all* the gods.

My altar.

My jaws of life

in the form of a warm-colored corpse

still living, still loving—

COOTI. For we are dead and alive

all at once, you and I.

We laugh at death.

It's been out of business

for many moons, that death.

FELO. Shut down.

COOTI. Out to lunch—permanently.

FELO. Your mouth to *your* ears.

COOTI. *(spanish)* Shh, espérate.

Es mi turno.

FELO. *(spanish)* Dale. *(portuguese)* Falar.

COOTI. *(spanish)* Yo te siento conmigo siempre...

aquí...

> *(touches his third eye)*

aquí...

> *(touches his mouth)*

y aquí.

   (touches the inside of his wrist)

FELO. *(smiles)*

COOTI. *(french)* Je t'aime.

FELO. *(portuguese)* E io te, bella.

COOTI. *How* did *I* get so lucky,

  to have married the bonniest lad in life?

  A potter with the softest kind of firm.

FELO. *(acknowledging his hands)* These small things?

COOTI. I love you like,

  like lungs do a benevolent breath.

  Like,

  like skin wraps itself round muscle

  and vessels.

  Sos mi primer beso.

  I can feel the atmosphere

  unfold the second I smell you.

  You are the perfect language we speak,

  made of a trillion tongues.

  Ticks and clicks.

  Sounds and boundless nouns.

  You,

  mi amor,

  are a computer.

FELO. A what?

COOTI. Mmhm.

FELO. Computer?

COOTI. The best kind.

God's kind.

With the holy O.S.

The kind man still struggles with to download its data from.

A complex simple.

You are a beautiful maze,

with walls made of sunflowers,

I will gladly get lost in for the rest of this daze.

FELO. My North Star.

COOTI. My road map

and a full tank of gas.

FELO. Let's take a nap!

COOTI. Let's!

> *(extremely excited, they both jump into the bed and get under the covers—heads still out)*

FELO. See you on the other siiiiiide.

COOTI. Last one there's the first one to rub the other's palms when we get back!

FELO. Deal!

> *(they fully cover themselves from head to toe. they go to sleep)*

Two

> *(while* **FELO** *and* **COOTI** *are sleeping,* **KAREN GOLD** *walks up to their front door)*

> *(she looks through the window and sees no one. she walks into the house)*

KAREN GOLD. Helloooooo.

Anybody herrrre?

> *(she looks around the house)*

> *(she begins to touch everything)*

> *(she sees the basket of tomatoes)*

Ooooh. Tomatoes!

> *(she walks over to where the basket is and picks a tomato up)*

> *(she bites into it)*

Eww!!

This tomato is so hot!

Gross!!!

> *(she throws it on the floor)*

> *(the tomato splatters all over)*

> *(she spits the bite she took onto the floor)*

> *(she wipes her mouth with her bare hand)*

> *(she picks up another tomato)*

Ow!

My hand!

This tomato is so cold!

What the fuck?

> *(she throws the tomato across the room, hitting a wall. it splatters all over)*

Who likes cold tomatoes?

> *(she rummages through the basket of tomatoes, throwing some on the floor and others wherever they land.)*

> *(after making a mess, she finally finds a tomato she approves of)*

Now *this* tomato is just right.

> *(she eats it)*

> *(there are tomato guts all over her face. juice and seeds dripping down her neck, forearms, and elbows)*

> *(this takes awhile)*

> *(she finishes)*

> *(she wipes her mouth with her bare hand. she walks around)*

I'm exhausted.

Is there like anywhere to rest here?

Hellooo?

> *(she sees a chair)*

> *(she sits in it)*

This chair is huge.

Who could rest on this thing?

(she sees a couch)

Ooh!

A couch.

That's just what I need.

(she works her way towards it)

(the chair breaks as she gets up)

(she doesn't acknowledge this)

(she lays on the couch)

Oh my god!

This couch is so *lumpy*.

Who would buy this kinda couch?

(she looks around)

I'm just so tired.

I've never been so tired in my life.

No one, I mean *no one* knows what it's like to be as tired as I am.

*(she sees the bed **FELO** and **COOTI** are safely sleeping in)*

A bed?

Okay, *now* we're talking.

(she takes her shoes off and throws them anywhere and everywhere. one of the shoes hits felo's freshly baked pinch pots and they come crashing down)

(she doesn't acknowledge this)

(she takes her socks off and tosses them as well)

(she heads towards the bed. the couch breaks as she gets up. she doesn't acknowledge this)

(she walks barefoot all over the tomatoes she splattered and spit on the floor)

(her feet get more disgusting with every step)

(she jumps onto the bed)

COOTI & FELO. OWWW!!!

KAREN GOLD. OH MY GOD!

FELO. WHAT THE?!

KAREN GOLD. WHAT ARE YOU DOING HERE?!

COOTI. WHAT ARE WE DOING HERE?!

FELO. THIS IS OUR HOUSE!

COOTI. *(acknowledging the mess all over)* OUR HOUSE!

FELO. YOU CRAZY?!

KAREN GOLD. Ohmygodohmygod okay.

Don't kill me, please. Please!

COOTI. Get off our bed! *Please!*

KAREN GOLD. I'll leave I'll leave okay.

Just please—

COOTI. My tomatoes!

KAREN GOLD. Don't kill me! HELP!

FELO. Why are you in our home?!

KAREN GOLD. I thought no one was here!

  HELP!

COOTI. And so you just break in?!

KAREN GOLD. Don't hurt me. I'll leave.

FELO. My pots!

COOTI. What did you dooo?!

KAREN GOLD. I'm leaving okay. Look—

FELO. Leaving?!

  Naaaaaah, mama.

    (**COOTI** *blocks* **KAREN GOLD** *from leaving*)

COOTI. Stay right there.

    (blackout)

Three

(the next day at the shrine's courthouse.
KAREN GOLD *stands before* **THE JUDGE***)*

THE JUDGE.   Ladies and gentlemen! Boys and girls! Animals and *animalettes*!

Thems, theys, others; LGBTQ-pluses, and non-gender-conforming-types!

Please, all rise for—well—*ME*!

> **(FELO** *and* **COOTI** *stand up.)*

> *(belting in laughter,* **THE JUDGE** *does a twirl to show off her glittery gown and sits)*

Okay, y'all sit.

Let's get this over with.

Miss Gold, I'm sure you can tell by how much more beautiful I am than you, that I have better things to do than to waste my afternoon on foolishness.

KAREN GOLD.   Judge this is not—

THE JUDGE.   It is *The Judge* Miss Gold.

The judger—not the judgee.

Here to judge *you*

so please *hush* for me.

Ooh, girl that rhymed.

KAREN GOLD.   This isn't fair! Look at that jury!

> **(FELO** *and* **COOTI** *are the only two sitting in the jury box)*

They don't look anything like me!

They look like—

THE JUDGE. Like what Miss Gold? Hmm?

Like what? What do *they* look like?

KAREN GOLD. Like… The Shrine?

Like they live in The Shrine?

THE JUDGE. That's cause they do.

As do I.

    (**THE JUDGE** *picks up her files*)

Miss Gold entered the dwellings of Felo and Cooti Brown without consent.

Because of these conditions, Miss Gold can be charged with Burglary in the First Degree, a felony charge, and can be sentenced to imprisonment for twenty years and a fine of $35,000.

KAREN GOLD. They could've killed me!

THE JUDGE. Miss Gold broke a chair, sofa, and Mr. Brown's pots which were handcrafted and *very* valuable. It will cost $500 to replace the chair, $1,000 for the couch, and $2,000 for the pots—

KAREN GOLD. That couch was horrendous—

THE JUDGE. *And* you can be charged with Criminal Damage to Property in the First Degree.

For this, Miss Gold you can receive an additional sentence of five years and a fine of $10,000.

KAREN GOLD. I was scared for my life!

THE JUDGE. Miss Gold *also* ate and ruined a basket of the most heavenliest tomatoes The Shrine has tasted?! Are you serious?! Maybe tomatoes aren't especially valuable where you're from—wherever that is. But *these* tomatoes *are*, and this is still considered *a crime*.

Miss Gold can be charged with Misdemeanor Theft

which carries a maximum penalty of ninety days in jail and a $1,000 fine because of this.

KAREN GOLD. I WILL ABSOLUTELY NOT!

THE JUDGE. KAREN!

>   *(rest)*

Gold.

>   *(rest)*

Miss Gold.

KAREN GOLD. Correct your honor! Miss *GOLD*.

THE JUDGE. *(a concerned face from* **THE JUDGE***)*

KAREN GOLD. That's right.

If I were you, *Judge*,

I would proceed with extreme caution in how you decide to evaluate this case.

>   *(acknowledging the jury box.)*

And how *you* reach your final verdict.

>   *(concerned faces from* **FELO** *and* **COOTI***)*

We wouldn't want things to get, umm, *lumpy.*

Would we now?

THE JUDGE. Oh.

>   *(beat)*

Uhh.

No.

>   *(beat)*

No, we wouldn't, Miss Gold.

We wouldn't want that.

>*(rest)*

Jury?

>*(**FELO** and **COOTI** slowly stand up)*

>*(**THE JUDGE** grabs the file with the verdict)*

THE JUDGE. In conclusion...

>*(**KAREN GOLD** brushes her tomato drenched hair behind her ears with her sticky fingers)*

THE JUDGE, FELO & COOTI. Girl you guilty.

KAREN GOLD. WHAT?!

THE JUDGE. Karen Gold, you will now be sentenced to twenty-five years and three months *not* in prison, but working in the tomato fields on the Felo and Cooti Brown estate.

KAREN GOLD. I demand to see your certification—

THE JUDGE. Ehh ehh ehh eh eh – until you have fully paid off your debt of $49,500 for damages and fines. Case closed.

(under her breath) Like ya mama's legs should've stayed.

>*(she smirks. gavel drops)*

Somebody come get this rude ass girl out my face, please.

End of Play

The Only Thing You Came to Hear

*Based on a True Story

By Thaddeus McCants

THE ONLY THING YOU CAME TO HEAR was first produced by Theater Masters via Zoom on May 20, 2021. The performance was directed by Dennis A. Allen II. The production stage manager was Kelly Martindale. The cast was as follows:

DOCK ELLIS . . . . Elisha Lawson

CHARACTERS

DOCK ELLIS – (Late twenties-early thirties) Black, Male-Identifying

Possible Additional Characters:

THE SKIPPER – (Sixties) White, Male-Identifying

THE GIRLFRIEND – (Twenties) Black, Female-Identifying

THE ROOKIE – (Twenties) Black, Male-Identifying

THE FINAL BATTER – (Thirties) Latinx, Male-Identifying

SETTINGS

One Baseball Card, Fresh from the Pack.

The Tarmac

Dock's L.A. Home

The Clubhouse

The Pitcher's Mound Olympus

Alone with just Your Thoughts.

TIME

1970

NOTES ON STAGING

Although text is delivered solely by Dock, this play is intended on being as fully staged as possible.

This is to say that while the play does not require anything at all, it may contain any number of additional actors or augmenting stagecraft.

(A baseball card drifts down from the sky. It looks old, it looks expensive.)

(Standing in tableau inside the card's brightly colored proscenium is a young Black man, DOCK ELLIS, in a 1970 Pittsburgh Pirates jersey. He stares forward with a welcoming – albeit intense – smile. A moment frozen in time.)

(Lights shift and DOCK comes to life. He steps out of the card and is suddenly in street clothes. Suddenly a real man. When he sees the audience, he peers over his nose for a moment before speaking directly to them.)

DOCK. You don't have to look at the stats on the back, by the way.

I'll just tell you.

Sometime y'all don't see us like we're real people.

As if you can't ask me a simple question.

I get it... I was larger than life.

They used to call me the Muhammad Ali of the Major Leagues.

I was too Black for Baseball.

They tell you that?

But y'all ain't come for that, did you?

Yeah... I know what you came for.

You bought my card so you must be a fan, so...

I guess I owe you the good one, right?

That's fine, I'll tell it, I'm not gonna tell it the way you want me to tell it,

But I'll tell you what happened.

Matter fact, we gotta go back two days before I even stepped foot on the mound... For what would be the defining moment of my career.

     Really, of my whole life.

But yeah... I'm from LA.

Born and raised.

And we had a game in San Diego.

So we flew in a few days before and as soon as we get off the plane...

     (**THE SKIPPER** *enters.*)

DOCK. I ask the Manager,

Or the Skipper as we call it baseball,

I ask him can I go home, to LA,

    'Cause we had an off day, you see what I'm saying?

Now, skipper was a good dude.

He was a ugly ass dude.

Two packs of chaw in his jaw at all times, spitting indoors, nasty as shit.

But he was a good dude.

Prolly calling me a Monkey behind my back.

    Or so I thought.

But he let me pitch, and he generally let me do my thing.

So I knew he was going to let me go home.

I knew it until the moment he told me he was NOT going to let me go home.

Even tho' we had an off day, you see what I'm saying?

He said "I was going to get into some mischief."

I said "nah skip.

I'll be good.

I'm just gonna go home and sleep."

And that was true, in its original intent.

The only issue with that was...

See, well I had...

Man, I mighta taken a little bit of LSD.

You know, right there on the tarmac before I had talked to Skip.

Fuck You!

Don't judge me.

I know it wasn't the best idea NOW.

But it was sitting in my bag looking all delicious

and I was assuming he was going to let me go home.

'Cause we had a Fucking Off Day! You understand what I'm trying to tell you?

So I took it,

'Cause I knew where it would hit me,

I'd be in own my little zone.

I'd be safe

I'd be home.

But it wasn't like that.

At. Fucking. All.

Instead we got a crisis on our hands.

'Cause it's T-Minus forty-five minutes-or-so before I'm tripping like bowlegged girl playing double dutch.

I'm about to be fucked up... In public.

And that's gonna be it for me.

See I was already on my last straw from some mischief I did earlier in the month.

So I pleaded.

I was on my knees I think.

And he said "Fine. But don't do no stupid shit."

And I said "Thank you!"

    And that I wouldn't do no stupid shit.

'Cause I had already done some stupid shit, you see what I'm saying?

And next thing I knew I was home.

The fuck knows how I got there...

    (THE GIRLFRIEND enters.)

DOCK. Now I got home and my girlfriend, or my fiancé at the time, she was later my wife but all those titles were short-lived if we're being honest with each other.

She answers the door and she looks at me for a second...

Says "The fuck is wrong with you?"

I said "I'm high as a Georgia Pine, fuck you mean?"

And she laughed and we went into her house...

Which was mine, I bought that shit, I just wasn't never there.

'Cause baseball ain't like it is now, we were on the road two-thirds of the year.

So she took care of the house when I was gone.

Looking back I don't even think we really liked each other too much,

But she always did drugs with me,

When I was feeling up,

    Or down,

        Or sad,

            Or anxious, which happened a lot those days.

Still does, if I'm being honest with you.

Matter fact I do miss her.

I been doing drugs for a long time

But nobody likes to do 'em alone, you know?

Makes you feel crazy when you're fucked up alone.

Makes you feel alone.

And who wants to feel that?

So I walked in the house and first thing I did,

Was start making smoothies,

'Cause I had just got money.

So I was eating all types of fresh fruits and shit.

We didn't have that shit growing up.

I didn't grow up in the hood.

But we still ain't wake up to strawberry banana.

That's some White people shit.

So I was fucked up.

I was dancing, drinking my little smoothie, and my life was good.

I was...

I was...

I was carefree.

For one of the first times, you know?

But you know that shit didn't last.

I woke up on the floor the next morning,

Which I thought was the next morning.

My Girl kicks me.

She says, "You better wake your ass up, you gotta pitch today motherfucker."

I said, "Pitch? Bitch, I pitch tomorrow."

'Cause I wasn't ready to pitch.

'Cause I had gotten up in the middle of the night and made another smoothie,

Put some more LSD in it.

So I was back up on that Georgia Pine.

Amongst the Gods in the stratosphere, you see what

I'm saying?

She grabbed the paper, threw it at me

Sure enough...there it is.

Starting Pitcher: Dock Fucking Ellis.

I looked at that shit in horror.

Like, "What the fuck happened to Yesterday?"

She laughed, said "I don't know, but you better get your ass to San Diego."

(**THE ROOKIE** *enters.*)

So I get into the clubhouse thirty minutes before the game stared.

And I start getting dressed.

I'm trying to play it cool but my buddy,

See we had a rookie on the team by the name of Dave Cash,

Good kid, he comes up to me,

And he tries to hand me three Greenies.

Now back in the seventies, Greenies was Dexamyl.

Which was a stimulant.

An Amphetamine.

Ninety percent of major league was on Dexamyl.

They won't tell you that.

But I will.

So Dave tries to give me three or four of them things. I told him, "I'm good." And he laughs, says "Nah, you pitching today.

I need you zinging."

I said No.

He said Yes.

I said No.

He said Yes.

I said No.

He said Why?

And I looked at him a long time.

But I couldn't tell him I was tripping on LSD.

So I took the pills.

I always take the pills.

And here we are...

On the mound in front of Ten Thousand people

And now I'm on Uppers,

I'm on Downers,

I'm on All-Arounders.

I am not OK.

This is going to be...

This is going to be something special.

And the Gods agreed, because right when I stepped up to the mound there was a mist.

It was like a fine mist over the whole stadium.

And I felt like the White dudes I seen in Gladiator movies.

I'm Spartacus up in this bitch...

I'm up on pitcher's mound Olympus.

And I remember thinking to myself, "I always want to feel like this."

Fucked up as I was, that cheering was why I was there.

That's why I wanted to make it to the Majors.

Why I worked so fucking hard to make to the Majors,

Well that and to prove my dad wrong.

I wanted to

...man I wanted to be significant.

What else is there to say, you know?

I wanted to be worth what it costs to feed my Black ass.

As my dad used to say.

And I did that.

I made it to the Major Leagues.

But once you're there.

Man, you'll do pretty much anything to stay there.

That's why all of us was taking drugs.

That's why I took more drugs than most.

To get that edge.

But fuck man, I didn't never mean to be on the mound on LSD.

Because LSD...if you don't know...is not a performance enhancing drug.

But I'm standing up there like I was the King of the world.

'Cause I didn't know no other way.

They used to call me the Muhammad Ali of Baseball.

I tell you that?

Well fuck you...so what if I did?

That was the prolly only time I liked what they said about me in the papers.

And I threw the first pitch.

Strike one...here we go.

Now the other team knew I was High.

But they didn't know what I was High on.

And I had this mean ass face on so they knew I meant business.

But inside I'm freaking out because I couldn't really see the batters.

I just knew if they were on the left side or the right side.

I had the catcher put tape on his fingers, so I could see the signals.

But that was it.

That was all I had to go on.

Other than that I was just throwing.

Ball one...

Strike four...?

The game continues...

And I wipe sweat from my brow.

And it's not the right color.

And I'm throwing.

And I'm throwing.

And I'm thinking it's going OK.

But I'm throwing a wild game.

I mean I'm hitting batters.

I'm throwing balls in the dirt.

And Skipper is looking at me crazy and I'm thinking I'm 'bout to get pulled.

But it's the third inning and Dave Cash...

You remember Rookie Dave, good kid, he gave me the uppers.

Fucked my whole day up.

He comes over to me, puts his glove up over his mouth so no one could see it.

Me included, so that was kinda scary.

And his voice sounded underwater when he said,

"Hey man, you got a No-No going!"

A No-Hitter.

Meaning no one has hit the ball off you, the entire game.

Which in baseball is obviously quite a feat.

But I'm fucked up so I said "yeah right."

'Cept he pointed up at the scoreboard.

And sure enough.

Dave was right... No-No.

Now again, it wasn't pretty.

Man, I had never caught the ball with two hands before.

'Cause I thought the ball was BIG as a beach ball.

But sometimes it was SMALL too.

And LSD is not helping me figure out which is which.

So it was going well.

But I wasn't in control.

Yet still.

Inning after Inning.

Dave Cash is looking at me.

"you STILL got a No-No going"

And you can feel the energy of the older guys on the team wanting to tell him to shut up.

'Cause it's a superstition where you're not supposed to talk about it when a guy is throwing a No-No.

But Rook wasn't that type of kid.

Kept saying "you got a No-No going."

"You throwing a No-No."

And he wasn't lying.

So we get to the final inning,

Skipper looks at me he said "Can you do it?

Can you finish it off?"

I said "Hell yeah, and quit calling me a Monkey all the time!"

He said "What?"

I said "Nevermind, I can do it!"

And I went out there and I struck two guys out in a row.

I had peaked in the seventh, now I was on a roll.

(THE FINAL BATTER *enters.*)

But here is the last batter.

Jerry Morales, surefire Hall of Fame guy.

And he looked pissed.

In his defense I hit him with a pitch earlier,

Almost hit him with two.

And dudes don't like getting plunked, I get that.

So I threw him a strike

I threw him a ball.

I threw him a pitch and he smacked the shit out of it.

Hit the fucking stuffing off the ball.

I thought that ball was going to hit the Moon.

But as I looked at it...

I realized the Moon was coming right at...

My Face.

I fell to the ground.

I closed my eyes.

I open my eyes.

Ball was in my glove.

Crowd.

Goes.

Bananas.

I thought to myself "I just scored a Touchdown."

Dave Cash said "You did it... You threw a No-No!"

I thought yeah, "I threw a No-No...on acid."

And I will forever be...

So goddamn embarrassed by that fact.

*(Everybody is gone. **DOCK** is alone again.)*

Because now that's all anybody wants to talk about.

That's the only thing y'all came to hear, right?

The rest of my life, that's it.

No-No this.

    LSD that.

They don't wanna talk about my work as an addiction counselor.

They don't talk about my work with young professional athletes.

My work with Sickle Cell...how I helped invent Free Agency.

You know how much money I put in athlete's pockets, doing what I did?

But you don't even know what I did.

You just want to talk about Acid.

And yeah it's fun. And it's funny.

But just 'cause it's funny don't make it a joke.

I always think about...

I think about how much I needed a fucking hug back then.

I think about if somebody would have just given me a hug at that point in my life,

At any point in my life,

How different I think things would have been.

Because it wasn't like I didn't care.

I cared TOO much.

I was terrified.

    Terrified of failure.

      Terrified to let my people down.

'Cause there really ain't but a few of us brothers who get a chance at one time.

So we gotta get it right.

    Right?

I would think about that every time I would fuck up,

Or every time I got fucked up.

And that's scary.

That's a lot of pressure.

Lot of responsibility.

But that's what it means to be a Black man right?

That everything you do yourself reflects upon the whole.

Because most of the time you're the only one in the room.

So yeah... I'm always kind of sorry people remember me for that.

'Cause I did a lot more.

Oh yeah, I even got a letter from Jackie Robinson, while I was playing.

And I don't want take too much more of your time.

I know you're all busy people.

Um, but I was flying off at the mouth to some White reporters, like I do.

And I got fined, and I got suspended.

And I'm sitting in my house drunk and sulking and...

And I got this express letter, Jackie was a old Nigga, sending telegrams and shit.

But what he wrote, Um...

What he wrote sort of sums up what it means to be Black.

I got the letter right here... He said, Uh...

Dear Dock,

I read your comments in the paper and I wanted you to know how much I appreciate your courage and honesty. In my opinion, progress for today's players will only come from this kind of dedication. I am sure you also realize the consequences. The news media, while knowing full well you are right and honest, will use every means to get back at you: "Blacks should not protest, as you are." They will say. There will be times when you will ask yourself is it worth it all? I can only say Dock, it is, even though you will want to yield in the long run.

Try not to be left alone.

Try to get more players to understand your views, and you will find great support.

You have made a real contribution. I again appreciate what you are doing.

Continued Success,

Jackie Robinson

Oh man, I never read it like that...

       Aww shit.

I never got to tell him thank you.

And I didn't make it much longer then he did.

And some of these Black folx won't make it past today, you see what I'm saying?

Man, I guess in that way being Black is like an LSD trip, ain't it?

Because we may be in the same game...

       But we ain't really on the same planet.

Are we?

> *(He steps back into the Baseball card, back into tableau, smiling the same intense – albeit welcoming – grin, but it's different somehow.)*

> *(Blackout.)*

End of Play

The Idiots

by Prashant Nashi

THE IDIOTS was first produced by Theater Masters via Zoom on May 19, 2021. The performance was directed by Sanaz Ghajar. The production stage manager was Kelly Martindale. The cast was as follows:

JAKE . . . . Daniel K. Isaac
SAVERIN . . . . Abraham Makany
KEVIN . . . . Dan Domingues
KYLE . . . . .Ephraim Lopez

CHARACTERS

JAKE – Thirties. Male/male-identifying. Queer. BIPOC.

SAVERIN – Thirties. Male. Cis. BIPOC.

KEVIN – Forties. Male/male-identifying. Queer. Any race/ethnicity.

KYLE – Forties. Male/male-identifying. Queer. Any race/ethnicity.

SETTING

A classy wedding reception. Table Seven.

TIME

Tomorrow

AUTHOR'S NOTES

Dialogue that lacks punctuation indicates a stream of consciousness.

A slash (/) indicates overlapping dialogue.

Ideally, Kevin and Kyle share similar physical features, in the way some couples weirdly look alike. Y'all know those people. But it's not a deal breaker.

This morning, Jake expected to have a pleasantly normal day. At the start of the play, we're in the middle of the worst moment of his life.

(A classy wedding reception. Table Seven.)

(JAKE points in abject horror at his phone on the table. SAVERIN tries to do damage control.)

SAVERIN. It's okay! We can figure this out!

JAKE. We can't figure it out.

SAVERIN. We can figure it out!

JAKE. There's nothing to figure out! I texted Kevin about Kevin! I meant to text my sister about the ex that's right over there, but I texted my ex...about him!

SAVERIN. It's fine – it happens!

JAKE. Does it?

SAVERIN. I'm sure to someone somewhere.

> *(JAKE screams – the kind when you find out the world ate the last brownie.)*

It'll be okay. What did you text?

> *(JAKE points to the phone. SAVERIN picks it up and reads.)*

Ohh this is – oh. Oh my. I'm not sure Verizon even allows its customers to text in such...graphic detail. Why would you even want to tell your sister this?

Hold up, you really say things like this? You can't even say nice things like this to me.

JAKE. Well I obviously have to leave how much does it cost to change one's name I've been wanting a career change so doing a whole "everything" change should hasten the process do me a favor write down everyone here you think I may be friends with on social media so I know who to unfriend and make a clean break with.

SAVERIN. You need to breathe.

JAKE. I need to get the fuck out of here is what I need to do.

SAVERIN. Imagine the worst thing that could come of this. At the very least, it won't be that.

JAKE. Kevin could show everyone he knows. It will end up on the internet. He'll tag my name, address, number, social security number, the fact that I have some controversial opinions on hummus. Then it'll...

(JAKE's *voice fades into the background.*)

(*The lights dim ever so slightly, transporting us to a dream-like state.*)

SAVERIN. Bruh. You're an idiot. For real, though, what's up with the ride-or-dies always being idiots? Thank gawd I'm the legit one. I mean, I told you time and time again: Double. Check. Your. Messages! Having The Fastest Fingers in the West may be good after midnight, but between the hours of nine and five, that shit will get you in trouble. This is peak-you...

...and I live for this. Listen. I got you. I mean, I have to because you obviously cannot be trusted with anything.

(*Lights up.* JAKE's *voice fades back in.*)

JAKE. ...and they'd plaster my face all over Times Square with the caption "this guy am I right????"

SAVERIN. (*Pretending to have heard it all.*) Oof. Yeah, what a bleak dystopia. What do you need me to do?

JAKE. I need you to steal his phone.

SAVERIN. Then what?

JAKE. We delete the message.

SAVERIN. Do you know his passcode?

JAKE. I need you to steal his phone so we can break his phone.

SAVERIN. That's what you want?

JAKE. Yes.

SAVERIN. Okay.

> (**SAVERIN** *exits.* **JAKE** *paces.*)

> (*The lights dim, transporting us back to a dream-like state.*)

JAKE. Saverin. You're an idiot, but you're my idiot. I mean, thank god I'm the legitimate one.

But you deal with my b.s. and I appreciate you. Actually, you're the only one who deals with my b.s.

Huh.

To be fair, my problems are far more interesting than yours. Like that one time you got scared that hip-hop passed you by. I stopped paying attention when you framed it as your Greatest Struggle.

(The Straights, they're not alright.)

But you were there in third grade, and you're here now...and I love that. Then again, you know where all the bodies are buried, so even if I wanted to get rid of you...

> (*Lights up.* **SAVERIN** *enters with two old-fashioneds.*)

SAVERIN. Here you go.

> (**SAVERIN** *casually takes a sip.* **JAKE** *waits.*)

Did you know Sophie and Tye are expecting? Just saw

them. They look great. Got matching highlights.

JAKE. Where's the phone?

SAVERIN. I didn't get it.

JAKE. Hm. I guess it is kind of hard to steal a phone. Let me think.

SAVERIN. No, I mean I didn't try.

JAKE. Why?

SAVERIN. I was thinking...we break the phone.

JAKE. Really happy to see you're keeping up here.

SAVERIN. Then what? We break it, then what?

JAKE. I dunno. Throw it away.

SAVERIN. Then what?

JAKE. We fucks with some appetizers.

SAVERIN. What about his iPad?

JAKE. We break it.

SAVERIN. By breaking into his hotel?

JAKE. Okay.

SAVERIN. And his computer.

JAKE. I get it.

SAVERIN. Then we red pill and join the machines and break into the cloud and erase all his data / then we blue pill and come back and we're like, "ohhh it was all a dream was that real I dunno let's get some pancakes."

JAKE. / Alright, I get it. I get it. I get it! I got it!

SAVERIN. You sent the text. He's going to read it. It's done.

JAKE. I know.

SAVERIN. There are worse things than an ex finding out you kept a few of their sweaters, you know?

(**KEVIN** and **KYLE** *stroll in.*)

KEVIN. *(To* **KYLE,** *then.)* I think this is our table – Jake? Saverin?

SAVERIN. Fuck.

JAKE. *(Aggressively over-the-top.)* Kevin! What a surprise! Great to see ya!

KEVIN. Wow! You, too.

SAVERIN. Fuuuck.

KEVIN. Saverin, you look great.

SAVERIN. Uh, you as well, as always. And this is...

KEVIN. Oh! My god, I'm so sorry. This is Kyle. Kyle this is Saverin and –

> (**JAKE** *aggressively thrusts his body across* **SAVERIN** *just to extend his arm for a handshake.)*

JAKE. – Jake! Great to meet you love your suit Tom Ford?

SAVERIN. Fuck.

> (**KEVIN** *and* **KYLE** *sit.* **SAVERIN** *supportively puts his hand on* **JAKE**'s *shoulder, and sits.)*
>
> (*An uncomfortable beat.*)
>
> (*Another uncomfortable beat.*)
>
> (*Oh my god why won't this beat end?*)

Anyone up for another drink?

JAKE. NO – um, sure. *(Trying to play it cool.)* Sure.

SAVERIN. *(Under his breath.)* Oh god. *(Then.)* Kevin?

KEVIN. A G&T would be great.

SAVERIN. Classic for a classy guy. Kyle, mind helping me? Wish I had more hands! Ha.

KYLE. Sure.

> (*As* **SAVERIN** *and* **KYLE** *walk away,* **SAVERIN** *gives* **JAKE** *a "keep it together!" look.* **JAKE** *actively avoids* **SAVERIN***'s eyes.*)

JAKE. How've you been?

KEVIN. Great. Great. Nothing too exciting. I moved to Rockford a few months ago.

JAKE. Rockford? Fancy. Did you hire yourself a gardener, maid, and professional ass-wiper, too?

KEVIN. Yes. Soon. And interviewing candidates on Monday.

> (*They share a genuine laugh. A beat.*)

JAKE. Okay. Extremely attractive elephant in the room. You probably saw that text...look, I was angry at how things ended with us, but I get it. I've moved on, holistically. But everything I said is...it's true.

I...wow OK... I still have feelings for...

> (**JAKE***'s voice fades. The lights dim again, transporting us back to a dream-like state.*)

KEVIN. It's crazy how attractive I am. Seriously.

I. Look. Great. A human Adonis.

Science should really inspect my bones and marvel at the harmony in which my skeleton operates like a goddamn perpetual motion machine.

It's crazy people get to be around me.

God. I am so lucky to be around me.

> (*Lights up.* **JAKE***'s voice fades back in.*)

JAKE. ...and I think that, if I could have a re-do, I'd take it. You know? But I get it.

So, uh, yeah. That's my piece. What do you think?

KEVIN. *(Pretending to have heard it all.)* Ha, yeah, totally. That's really funny.

JAKE. Funny?

> *(**JAKE**, confused. **SAVERIN** and **KYLE** come back, drinks in hand. They laugh like the best of friends.)*

SAVERIN. Jake! Remember how I applied to the Senior Asset Manager spot at McKendry Williams?

Guess who their hiring manager is!

KYLE. Well I don't have final say or anything, but I'm going to make sure his resumé is at the top.

SAVERIN. Kyle, my man. Seriously, we should chill sometime.

KEVIN. That's so great – look at us being mature adults!

Hey, did you see Sophie and Tye? Those highlights? Good-ness gra-cious.

> *(A beat. **JAKE**, confused. **KEVIN**, oblivious. **SAVERIN** and **KYLE**, having a great time.)*

Oh, did they just bring out hummus crostinis? High in protein – what a flex.

Save our seats?

SAVERIN. Of course.

> *(**KEVIN** and **KYLE** exit.)*

Kyle, really cool dude. *(Off of **JAKE**'s expression.)* Whoa, hey you okay?

JAKE. I just bared my soul, and he said, "That's funny."

SAVERIN. What do you mean?

JAKE. I brought up the text. I was honest. Really honest. "That's funny."

SAVERIN. You mean he didn't –

JAKE. – I went full "dear diary," and no reaction. That's weird, right?

> (SAVERIN *slowly builds to a rage only a best friend can have.* JAKE *matches the intensity.*)

SAVERIN. What??

JAKE. Yeah.

SAVERIN. WHAT.

JAKE. RIGHT?

SAVERIN. You bled for him and he goes, "Heh"??

JAKE. I spoke of the graphic detail, graphically.

SAVERIN. What the – Jake, you're the bravest person I know.

JAKE. Thank you!

SAVERIN. Did you hear the way he said "G&T"? It's called gin and tonic. What, are you from Cork or some shit? The pretense!

JAKE. Such pretense!

SAVERIN. And that guy, Kyle. What a stupid name. <u>Kyle</u>.

JAKE. Kyle.

SAVERIN. Kyyyyle.

JAKE. Kyleeee.

SAVERIN. K y l e.

JAKE. Gross. It was almost like he didn't know what I was talking about.

(Huh. That thought settles in. They take out their phones, check for a signal.)

SAVERIN. I don't have many bars.

JAKE. I don't have any.

SAVERIN. Huh. So that text never...

*(A thoughtful beat. **SAVERIN** reaches into his pocket, grabs his car keys, tosses them to **JAKE**.)*

Get my car ready. I'll get his phone and find out what hotel he's in. I have golf clubs in the trunk. An iron will do more damage.

JAKE. Hey. Sav. Thanks. For... Yeah.

SAVERIN. Always, bruh.

End of Play

(Un)Scripted

By Dave Osmundsen

(UN)SCRIPTED was first produced by Theater Masters via Zoom on May 20, 2021. The performance was directed by Sanaz Ghajar. The production stage manager was Kelly Martindale. The cast was as follows:

MIRANDA . . . . Tal Anderson
PROMPTER . . . . Eileen Seeley
RANDY . . . . Imran W. Sheikh

CHARACTERS

MIRANDA – (Nineteen) A young Autistic woman

PROMPTER – A female voice; should have a strong vocal quality

RANDY – (Nineteen) A young neurotypical man

(A coffee shop (or what looks like one). **RANDY**, *nineteen, wearing a cap and an apron, stands behind the register.* **MIRANDA**, *nineteen, enters and walks to the counter. She wears a slightly forced but still friendly smile. She walks with a well-suppressed nervous energy.* **RANDY** *greets her.)*

RANDY. Hi, welcome to Coffee Cups! What can I get for you?

MIRANDA. Hi, yes, may I have a medium iced vanilla latte with whipped cream?

RANDY. *(Taking a cup.)* You certainly may! And who will this be for?

MIRANDA. It will be for Miranda.

RANDY. Miranda. Got it! Will there be anything else?

MIRANDA. Ummmm...

> *(**MIRANDA** doesn't know what to say next. She is silent for an uncomfortably long time. We hear a **PROMPTER** – a soothing, yet no-nonsense feminine voice.)*

PROMPTER. Miranda? What do you say when the barista asks if there will be anything else?

MIRANDA. *(Faces the audience. Mounting anxiety.)* Sorry. This part always throws me off. I can't decide if I want the oatmeal raisin cookie or the rice krispie treat or the cake pop or the –

PROMPTER. You know you don't have to have any of those things. The script says –

MIRANDA. *(More mounting anxiety.)* The script says to pick one of them or none of them but I don't know which one to pick if I am to pick one because there are so many and ordering something or nothing might affect how the rest of the scene goes and what if I end up wanting one more than the other and –

PROMPTER. Breathe, Miranda. Breathe.

MIRANDA. *(Takes a deep breath. Then another. Then continues.)* OK. Then can I have the...

> *(Silence. One second crawls by. Then another...)*

RANDY. May I suggest the rice krisp –

PROMPTER. Let her decide, Randy.

> *(...then another.* **MIRANDA** *turns to the* **PROMPTER**.*)*

MIRANDA. I'm sorry, can we start over? I know it by heart, I promise I know it by heart. I was practicing this script with my mom all last night and we had it down cold except for this part because I didn't know what I was going to want until I was actually doing the module. Can we please start over?

PROMPTER. All right. You have two more tries then, Miranda.

MIRANDA. Yes I know. I will get it right. I promise.

PROMPTER. Let's take it from the top.

RANDY. *(To the* **PROMPTER**.*)* Maybe we should take a few minutes? Just for her to calm –

MIRANDA. No. I just want to do this. I know I got this. From the top. Take Two!

> *(***MIRANDA*** *exits.)*

PROMPTER. Whenever you're ready, Miranda.

(**MIRANDA** *enters the coffee shop. Her smile is a bit more forced and anxious than before. Her nerves are slightly less oppressed.*)

RANDY. Hi, welcome to Coffee Cups! What can I get for you today?

(**RANDY** *takes a cup.*)

MIRANDA. Hi, yes, may I have a medium iced vanilla latte with whipped cream?

RANDY. You certainly may.

MIRANDA. Miranda's my name. In case you – Wait. No! UGH! THAT'S NOT THE LINE! I'm sorry, really I'm sorry, I know I'm supposed to wait until the barista asks my name, but I got nervous and jumped ahead –

RANDY. It was my fault. I picked up the cup too soon. That threw her off.

PROMPTER. That's OK, Randy. Mistakes happen. Miranda, take a deep breath.

(**MIRANDA** *takes a very deep breath.* **RANDY** *almost whispers to her.*)

RANDY. It's OK. People typically need more than one try at this module. You're doing great.

MIRANDA. You're *typical*. You don't have to try *at all*.

PROMPTER. Let's take it back to "You certainly may."

RANDY. You certainly may! And who will this be for?

MIRANDA. It will be for Miranda.

RANDY. Miranda. Got it! Will there be anything else?

(*Long, agonizing pause.* **MIRANDA** *turns towards the* **PROMPTER.**)

MIRANDA. I'm sorry. The whole scene is thrown off. Can we please start over?

PROMPTER. This will be your last try, Miranda.

MIRANDA. I know. I want to get it right. *Really right.*

PROMPTER. All right. Let's start again.

(**MIRANDA** *exits.*)

Whenever you're ready.

(**MIRANDA** *enters. Her smile is even more anxious and forced than the last time. She is doing her darndest to keep her cool!*)

RANDY. Hi, welcome to Coffee Cups! What can I get for you?

MIRANDA. Hi, yes, may I have a medium iced vanilla latte with whipped cream?

RANDY. *(Taking a cup.)* You certainly may! And who will this be for?

MIRANDA. It will be for Miranda.

(**RANDY** *writes her name on the coffee cup.*)

RANDY. Mi-ran-da... Would you like anything else?

MIRANDA. Can I have a...

...

...

...

Rice... krispie treat... please?

RANDY. Absolutely! Anything else?

MIRANDA. No thank you.

RANDY. That'll be six dollars and ninety-three cents.

MIRANDA. Alright!

(**MIRANDA** *pulls out some dollar bills and*

change and, taking her sweet time, counts to ninety-three cents. She gives the change to **RANDY**.)

MIRANDA. Here you go. Six dollars and ninety-three cents!

RANDY. Exact change! We love customers like you!

MIRANDA. Yes, I want to get rid of as many coins as possible.

RANDY. Usually I want to *keep* as many coins as possible. So I don't run out of them too quickly.

(*Five or so seconds pass. Suddenly,* **MIRANDA** *laughs.*)

MIRANDA. That's funny! "We love customers like you."

RANDY. Yeah! Ha ha...

Your latte and rice krispie treat will be right out.

MIRANDA. Thank you. Have a nice day!

RANDY. You too!

(*The scene has ended.* **MIRANDA** *throws her hands up.* **RANDY** *applauds.*)

MIRANDA. I did it! I did it I did it I got through the scene!!!

PROMPTER. Good job, Miranda. Randy, you can take ten before the next student.

RANDY. Got it. Good job, Miranda!

(**RANDY** *exits.*)

MIRANDA. When do I get the script for the next module? I know it's about humor and making jokes and being funny! I love being funny! I can't wait to get started!

PROMPTER. I'm sorry, Miranda. You won't be moving on to that module.

(Silence. **MIRANDA** *registers this.)*

MIRANDA. What? But why?

PROMPTER. There are *three* things that show me you're not ready to move forward in your social improvement.

MIRANDA. But I thought I had this script down cold!

PROMPTER. It wasn't your knowledge of the script, Miranda. You clearly knew it very well. However, you stumbled on the improv bit, where you had to pick a food item. The humor script has several more improv bits, and I fear you may find it more of a challenge than you're ready for.

MIRANDA. I know I tripped up, but I can get better. If you give me another chance –

PROMPTER. My second note has to do with the exact change. We provided you with a ten dollar bill you could've given Randy, like typical people would.

MIRANDA. But I like giving exact change because the cashiers run out of coins and –

PROMPTER. One person digging for exact change just holds up the line, and you don't want to be holding up a line of caffeine addicts in the real world. We went over this in our self-awareness module, remember?

MIRANDA. But cashiers would have to count the coins they give back to us anyway –

PROMPTER. Finally, there was your reaction to Randy's joke.

MIRANDA. Was that "We love customers like you"? I *did* laugh at that!

PROMPTER. Moments after the fact. People want to know their jokes are funny right away. They have to know that you found it funny.

MIRANDA. But I *did* find it funny! Please, if you just give me the humor script I could –

PROMPTER. That's my feedback. You can either repeat one of the previous modules, or try this one again in a month. But right now, we have to get ready for the next student.

>   (**MIRANDA** *gets down on her knees.*)

MIRANDA. Please, I'm *imploring* you, let me try again. I worked so hard to get to this point. I got through the introducing myself module, the asking questions module, the restaurant module, the public transportation module –

I *know* I can do the humor module, please!!!

PROMPTER. You're just not ready, Miranda. I'm sorry.

Now I'm not going to ask you one more time. We need to get ready for the next student.

>   (*We hear the* **PROMPTER** *putting her microphone down. We hear her walking away. A moment.* **MIRANDA** *hangs her head, dejected.* **RANDY** *enters, having overheard a good part of the last conversation. He sets a coffee cup by* **MIRANDA**.)

MIRANDA. I don't even like coffee. I prefer tea.

RANDY. This *is* tea.

MIRANDA. Thank you.

>   (**MIRANDA** *takes the cup.*)

RANDY. You're welcome. You did really well, that last time, I thought...

You know, I've been doing this for like a year now. I've never seen anyone as dedicated to social improvement as you. I mean, the discipline you show in memorizing these scripts. I haven't really seen it in anyone else who does this program.

...

Hey, you know what I just realized? My name is *Ran*dy. Yours is Mi*ran*da.

(**MIRANDA** *sips her tea.*)

MIRANDA. Must be so great, being typical. You get to say whatever you want and people don't care if you're following the script or if you're going too fast or too slow.

RANDY. Oh, people care. *Trust* me. I used to work at a coffee shop – like, an *actual* coffee shop – and my first day at the register, the first order I took was from this business guy in like a suit and everything. He gave me his order, but I was so overwhelmed by the buttons on the register that I just forgot. I asked him to repeat his order, and he said, "*Caramel macchiato*, are you deaf?!" Like, *sorry* for wanting to get your order right, you know?

(**MIRANDA** *sips her tea.*)

RANDY. Look. Honestly. The scripts they give you here. They're basic. They say you need to learn them to get by in the typical world, but they only reflect like, a *fraction* of it. And you seem like you get on just fine. In your own way.

MIRANDA. In my own way, I never know what to say. I'm always scared I'll say the wrong thing. Or make people feel weird. Or make them think I'm weird. These scripts are the only way I can make sure what I'm saying is worth saying. Right now, I don't have a script, so I don't even know where or how this sentence should end.

RANDY. You're doing fine to me. Better than the crap they give you to memorize here.

(*A second crawls by. Then another. Then* **MIRANDA** *laughs. Loud and long.*)

MIRANDA. Sorry, I just got your joke!

RANDY. It's not a joke, it's true, the scripts they give you here are crap!

MIRANDA. No, not that.

Randy.

Miranda.

Ran.

I just got it. Ha ha. You're funny.

RANDY. Why thank you. See? You don't need a script to know what's funny or not. Just go with your instinct. Like you just did.

MIRANDA. In that instant I didn't need a script. But other situations. With other people... I'm never sure.

I just want to be *sure.*

> (**RANDY** *nods. A moment of unscripted connection.*)

End of Play

blooms

By a.k. payne

blooms was first produced by Theater Masters via Zoom on May 19, 2021. The performance was directed by Dennis A. Allen II. The production stage manager was Kelly Martindale. The cast was as follows:

LETICIA .... Nora Carroll

KIM ....Sharina Martin

CHARACTERS

LETICIA – Black non-binary femme, late twenties, she/they

KIM – Black woman, late twenties, she/her

(A bus pulls up in front of a grocery store. **LETICIA** *and* **KIM** *disembark and watch the bus rumble away. They both wear blue vests.* **KIM** *lights a cigarette. It's early morning. It's quiet in a gentle way and spring in a blooming way and not too hot and not too cold in a way that makes you wanna stand outside and drink the day long as you are able. And you are able till the clock strikes seven. At seven you clock in, the earth shakes and there goes your freedom.)*

LETICIA. i'm in love with you

KIM. everybody in love with me

LETICIA. i can't do this shit forever, kim. a year of my life and we just fuckin around w time?

i said i love you.

KIM. what you want back, leticia?

LETICIA. forget it

(She starts towards work.)

KIM. how long we got?

*(**LETICIA** halts.)*

LETICIA. 6:50. Ten minutes.

(Beat, **KIM** *nods, puts out her cigarette.* **KIM** *don't put out her cigarette for nobody.)*

KIM. you know how chelle thinks she's the shit cause she got promoted to assistant manager after working here for a month?

LETICIA. what, kim?

KIM. bear with me.

raheem said he just thinks her ass is fat and secretly is hoping she'll fuck him in the bread aisle after her shift. that's what he told tyrone in the break room.

LETICIA. raheem thinks everybody's ass is fat.

KIM. this different. raheem think she's gonna be his wife. i caught him writing mrs. michelle lewis in the corner of an expense report when i walked in his office to tell him about a rat i saw in produce. he made me promise not to tell nobody. he thinks if anybody knew he wanna do more than fuck chelle for her fat ass he'd lose respect as manager, as a man.

he ain't say nothing about love in the break room

i ain't never believed in it

but in that moment i was like damn

raheem, the manager who won't talk about love in the break room he manages

like even when we got some power we still afraid.

so what that say about the powerless?

what that say about you and me? –

LETICIA. *(A whisper.)* i mean it, kim

KIM. – raheem would rather talk about chelle's fat ass than face himself

people liars generally

and full of shit usually

and we all too scared to be real you know –

LETICIA. *(A whisper.)* i'm tryna be real wit you.

KIM. – and i'm not bout be giving my heart away

in a world full of liars

(**LETICIA** *nods.*)

LETICIA. then take your shit

today after our shift

i stopped lying a long time ago

life too short and if you knew me at all, you'd know

so

take your shit

go

a year of my life

i'm not gon keep fuckin around w time.

KIM. *(A plea.)* i wouldn't believe myself either

LETICIA. forget it kim.

KIM. nah just hear me. please.

i think all that self love shit is for the birds

i think it's just selfishness wrapped up to look pretty

i think we want things

like i know i want you.

like i think we want a world where love exists

i don't think we in it

i think what we perform and what we are ain't all that
different

i think raheem talking about chelle like she just a piece
of ass

don't get cancelled out

by him dreaming about her being his wife in secret

by him dreaming about love in private

LETICIA. i think we all just trying our best, kim

i think the powerless know more about love

than the powerful

i think we got to

i don't think love about being neat

i think love is all entangled up with wanting

i think they twins, best friends or cousins

i don't think raheem lewis is of the powerful

he scared

i'm scared too

you run around pretending like you ain't scared

like you impenetrable

you soft, kim

we all need a second to be soft

    (Beat.)

how long we got

KIM. 6:55. five minutes.

LETICIA. okay

okay

so

give me these five minutes

let me convince you that it exists

if i don't...we walk in there

we do our shift

and you go home and take your shit

we wash our hands of alla this

    (Beat.)

KIM. *(A whisper.)* five minutes.

LETICIA. when you eat soup you use a spoon that's way too small for soup

KIM. *(A laugh, in spite of herself.)* what

LETICIA. you use that tiny spoon

it makes no sense

it makes me laugh

when you wake up in the morning you always got crust in the exact same places

i don't know how it happens

it's like your body remembers

and draws this map on your face

i spent months thinking i was tripping

i'm not tripping

crust in the corner of your left eye

in the corners of your mouth

on your right eyelash

a streak down your left cheek

your wear that green sweater when you feeling sad

you hate those boots but you won't throw them away because they remind you of home you feel like this job is stealing your spirit away.

i know because every time we get off the bus you close your eyes like you praying.

it's like half a second but i feel it cause your breath is different.

your breath is like your breath when you see art that's really bad, it's like your breath when you say

KIM & LETICIA. global warming

antiblackness

and capitalism

and this what we dreaming

LETICIA. you won't leave cause the money pays more than tryna make the art that makes your breath light.

you won't leave cause you think it's too late.

you won't leave cause you're scared of ending up like your mom.

you won't leave cause of me which i think is stupid but i couldn't tell you that without telling you i love you too. i love you too.

you starting to like your hair. you sometimes catch yourself in the mirror and think who is thaaaaat but then you stop yourself and divert your gaze and it's super cute and i wish you'd stare at yourself longer.

you hate being called beautiful, you think most words are empty, especially adjectives. you prefer being held.

sometimes you talk in your sleep about how terrible you are at making pancakes.

you are terrible at making pancakes.

KIM. you burn water

LETICIA. i just be forgetting sometimes

let me be

> *(Laughter curls up around them.)*

> *(Tears in the corners of KIM's eyes.)*

> *(A beat.)*

KIM. i saw something in raheem's eyes that day in his office

when he caught me looking at the corner of the expense report

something like a plea not to tell nobody there's parts of me

that want more than this grocery store

or a plea not to tell nobody that we all

get weak sometimes

and start thinking about places where we might be soft

before we get back to stacking cans of tuna

or counting paper bags to see how many more got to be ordered

with the next delivery always looking to the next delivery

> *(As the delivery truck rumbles up before the store.)*

LETICIA. mondays

6:59 am

on the dot

cause the delivery truck driver

loved being in the military

'fore he was dishonorably discharged

for punching a sgt

after they called him a nigger

during PT

KIM. he'll tell anyone who listens

so they put some respect

on his name so he can stand

up

a little taller

a plea

LETICIA. before we get back to our own rightful place in the world

KIM. on register three

LETICIA. shirt tucked in khakis

KIM. blue vest neatly pressed

LETICIA. a smile that says welcome

to save a lot

where you can save a lot

KIM. before we

erase the corners

and hope the pink dust

reaches somebody

with some power

to rearrange the world

(Beat.)

i love you too, leticia.

(From somewhere, pink dust begins to fall. Maybe it is pollen. Maybe it is magic... A bus rumbles into the stop. A beat. They look at each other. **KIM** *takes off her blue vest and hands it to* **LETICIA**. *They kiss each other a kiss that got some dreams entangled in it, a kiss that say we in this, together.* **KIM** *boards the bus.* **LETICIA** *looks directly at you.* **LETICIA** *walks to work.)*

end of play

Sahi Vaqt Pe *or* The One with the Biological Clock

By Ankita Raturi

SAHI VAQT PE OR *THE ONE WITH THE BIOLOGICAL CLOCK* was first produced by Hypokrit Theatre Company (Arpita Mukherjee, Artistic Director; Molly Houlahan, Associate Artistic Director) as part of Tamasha: A South Asian Performing Arts Festival at The Players Theatre in New York, New York on February 8, 2019. The performance was directed by Charlotte Murray. The stage manager was Peter Royston. The cast was as follows:

INA . . . . Krushika Patankar

SUMAIRA . . . . Piyali Syam

SHOPKEEPER . . . . Rohan Gurbaxani

SAHI VAQT PE OR *THE ONE WITH THE BIOLOGICAL CLOCK* was then produced by Theater Masters via Zoom on May 19, 2021. The performance was directed by Sanaz Ghajar. The production stage manager was Kelly Martindale. The cast was as follows:

INA . . . . Brinda Dixit

SUMAIRA . . . . Sara Haider

SHOPKEEPER . . . . Mueen Jahan

CHARACTERS

INA – Indian-American woman, late twenties, bisexual, speaks a mile a minute

SUMAIRA – Pakistani-American woman, late twenties, lesbian, a listener, a planner

SHOPKEEPER – Indian-American man, late forties, always adds his two cents

SETTING

A bodega in NYC.

AUTHOR'S NOTES

When presenting this play for a primarily English-speaking audience: please do not provide translations. Do not translate the Hindi/Urdu into English or the English into Hindi/Urdu. Please *do* provide subtitles or closed captioning for the Deaf and hard-of-hearing communities. These should be in whichever language is being spoken, and in Romanized script throughout as it appears in the text. Do not use Devanagari or Nastaliq script unless you plan to use all three scripts together. Please do not simply omit the Hindi/Urdu from the subtitles or closed captioning.

(An **INDIAN MAN** *sits behind the counter at an otherwise deserted bodega on a Manhattan street-corner. We hear a clock ceaselessly ticking the time away.)*

*(***TWO YOUNG SOUTH ASIAN WOMEN** *enter, mid-conversation. One of them (***INA***) starts pulling junk food and ice cream off the shelves at random as she talks, and she talks a lot, while the other (***SUMAIRA***) listens and quietly puts everything back on the shelves.* **INA** *doesn't notice; she's much too busy venting.)*

INA. So I finally hang up the phone and I'm in a really bad mood because I basically just yelled at my mom, which like shit why did I do that, but I need to calm down, right? So I say, okay I'll watch an episode of *Friends.*

SUMAIRA. You could've called me.

INA. I needed to calm down first.

SUMAIRA. Yeah you seem super calm.

INA. Shut up, it usually works. And I know if you watch *Friends* now it's actually kinda homophobic. Even though they basically had the first lesbian wedding ever on TV. I think. I'm not actually sure about that. Oh my god what was I even talking about?

SUMAIRA. Your mom.

INA. Right. Okay so I hang up on her like basically mid-sentence, like I have never done that before, I've never actually hung up on my mom. I mean sure I've put the phone on speaker and muted myself and turned on the TV so she can get all her shaadi talk out of her system. But I've never actually hung up on her like that. Like

INA. she knows. And now, I have to be the one to apologize because that's going to be the only thing that matters anymore.

SUMAIRA. Why'd you hang up?

INA. Oh my god, Sumaira, she was in the middle of saying biological clock for like the thirty-seventh time and I just did it. I didn't even think about it. And it felt kind of good? But then I was like fuuuuuuckkkkkk. And I'm like okay I need to calm down.

And I know I've seen *Friends* a million times already. And yeah any other show that is that white is like a hard pass for me. But it still makes me laugh.

SUMAIRA. Your mom didn't call you back?

INA. No, I think she's probably still seething. She's probably already gossiping with all the Delhi aunties about how insolent her daughter is. I'm completely screwed.

SUMAIRA. You're not. I'm sure we can fix this.

> (INA *pauses in the middle of picking out an*
> *Arizona Iced Tea from a fridge, and looks at*
> SUMAIRA. *She smiles.*)

INA. Maybe.

SUMAIRA. So you turn on *Friends*.

INA. Right. And it's totally random, but Netflix was like "keep watching" or whatever, and I happened to be on that episode where Paolo hits on Phoebe even though he's dating Rachel and Carol finds out the sex of the baby? And like everyone finds out the sex of the baby before Ross because he doesn't want to know?

SUMAIRA. Well, that's just bad luck.

INA. Actually no, not at first. Because I didn't even realize. Like I'm just watching this episode, laughing. And it actually was making me feel better for a little while.

But then at the end of the episode, Rachel dumps Paolo and he leaves and Rachel's like ugh I'm so done with men, which like wow relatable –

SUMAIRA. Men *are* the worst.

INA. Men are *totally* the worst. That's pretty much why I'm with you now.

SUMAIRA. That's why you're with me?

INA. No! Obviously –

SUMAIRA. Wow.

INA. Come on you know I didn't mean it like that. I was kidding. I mean... I'm sorry.

SUMAIRA. Whatever, you didn't mean it.

INA. I didn't mean it.

SUMAIRA. You were saying.

INA. Are you sure?

SUMAIRA. Yeah. *(...)* Seriously, Ina, it's fine. *(...)* So, Rachel says she's done with men, and then?

INA. Right. Okay, so Rachel is like I need to focus on myself and figure out what I want and then Ross is like, well not all guys are gonna be like Paolo.

SUMAIRA. You know I've seen this episode right?

INA. Okay yeah fine but listen this is the part that made me panic. So he says not every guy is gonna be a Paolo. And she says I know and I'm sure your little boy isn't gonna grow up to be one. And the whole tone of the scene changes, right? Ross is like wait I'm having a boy? And Rachel is trying to backpedal but it's done so they start yelling and celebrating. And the whole episode started with him having read all these baby books so like fuck I should have known you know, but it took me completely by surprise. And I'm sitting there

INA. watching this episode I've seen a hundred times before and I am crying. I'm fucking crying. And then I look at my phone, which is still lying where I threw it after hanging up on my mom and I'm like well fuck.

SUMAIRA. Shit.

INA. Yeah.

SUMAIRA. You were just riled up from the conversation with your mom. Like anything probably would have made you cry at that point.

INA. No, I think... I mean I wasn't...angry. Or sad. I was... I dunno, not happy. I was...like I was feeling what they were feeling. It was like, I dunno, like my uterus was crying.

SUMAIRA. Your uterus was crying?

INA. Okay I know it doesn't make any sense, but I guess I... I guess my uterus wants –

SUMAIRA. Nope. No. You were just telling me about your five-year plan literally yesterday.

INA. Yeah, but –

SUMAIRA. And it lines up with my five-year plan, Ina.

INA. I know, but –

SUMAIRA. We are making junior partner together.

INA. We can still –

SHOPKEEPER. Excuse me?

INA. Yes?

SHOPKEEPER. You are buying anything?

INA. Yeah...? Oh. Sumaira where's all the stuff we picked up?

SUMAIRA. I put it back.

INA. You put it back?

SUMAIRA. I was saving you from yourself.

INA. Oh. Thank you?

SHOPKEEPER. So...yes or no?

SUMAIRA. Yes or no what?

SHOPKEEPER. Hai bhagwan! What you are buying?

SUMAIRA. Oh. Sorry. One minute. Ina, what are you getting?

INA. Nothing apparently.

SUMAIRA. Let's get some ice cream.

INA. I don't need saving anymore?

SUMAIRA. The best way to save you changed when your uterus grew tear ducts and you lost sight of your future.

(INA walks off in a huff to find ice cream.)

SHOPKEEPER. From India?

SUMAIRA. Pakistan.

SHOPKEEPER. Oh Pakistan. Good good. I am India.

INA. India nahi Indian.

SHOPKEEPER. Arre vah! Hindi aati hai aap dono ko.

SUMAIRA. Urdu.

SHOPKEEPER. Haan haan. Ek hi to cheez hai na?

INA & SUMAIRA. Nahi.

SHOPKEEPER. Aap bhi Pakistan se hai?

INA. India.

SHOPKEEPER. Pata ta! Pata ta. India kahan?

INA. Dilli.

SUMAIRA. Hum chalein?

SHOPKEEPER. Oh haan ji, bilkul ji. $4.59 ji.

> (**INA** *gives him a five-dollar bill. Her phone rings. She answers without looking.*)

INA. Hello? *(Mouths "shit.")* Hi Ma.

Haan meh teekh hoon.

Nahi galti se –

Nahi Ma mein keh rahi hoon na galti –

Ohooo –

Ma hum do minute keh liye yeh shaadi aur bachein vaali baatein chhod sakte hain?

Sirf do minute, please I'm begging you!

Kyun?

> (*She looks at the* **SHOPKEEPER** *for change. He has it, but is politely waiting for her phone call to end to give it to her.*)

Arre Ma chhod bhi lo kabhi.

Nahi karni mujhe shaadi!

Nahi Ma mera matlab –

> (**INA** *gestures for* **SUMAIRA** *to take the change.* **SUMAIRA** *is not getting the sign language.* **INA** *is visibly frustrated.*)

Shayad Ma, shayad, lekin aaj nahi.

Voh toh shaadi ke bina bhi ho sakte hai na?

Oho meri Ma!

> (*She gives up on trying to leave and sits down right in the middle of the bodega.* **SUMAIRA** *and the* **SHOPKEEPER** *stare, baffled.*)

Okay, okay, sorry.

Phirse biological clock? Yeh aapka bhi biological clock chal raha he kya ki aap mujhe irritate kare bina chhod nahi sakti? Twenty-five pe bacchein, forty-five pe menopause, aur fifty-five pe apni beti ka sar khane lag jao?

> *(Ina's mother is audibly yelling (we can maybe make out a few words, like "sharam" or "izzat" or "biological clock" yet again).* **INA** *holds the phone away from her ear.* **SUMAIRA** *takes it and unceremoniously hangs up.* **INA** *is shocked.)*

INA. Oh good. Now I've hung up on her twice.

SUMAIRA. Ina, look at yourself. You're probably sitting on cat piss. Your mom can wait.

> *(***INA*** *gets up off the floor.)*

SHOPKEEPER. Ek baat kahoon?

INA. Kahiye.

SHOPKEEPER. Your mother is right.

INA. You don't even know what she said!

SHOPKEEPER. Biological clock is real.

SUMAIRA. Not you too.

SHOPKEEPER. Nahi sach, meh keh raha hoon.

SUMAIRA. Accha aap keh rahe hain? Phir toh sach hi hoga. Aap toh sab kuch jaante hain.

SHOPKEEPER. Nahi ji. Aisi koi baat nahi hai ji. Lekin biological clock toh hai. Mene dekha hai. Abhi shayad aap nahi jaanti, lekin sahi vaqt pe jaan lengi aap. Yeh loh ji, your change.

> *(He puts the change on the counter in front of* **INA**, *who hardly notices.)*

SUMAIRA. Let's go, Ina.

INA. What do you mean sahi vaqt pe?

SHOPKEEPER. Soch lo. Kabhi na kabhi toh dil karega.

SUMAIRA. Dil kare aur mann na kare toh?

SHOPKEEPER. Dil ki jeet honi hai ji. Meri behen ko dekh lo. Ek din uski puri zindagi hi badal gayi baccha paida karne ke peeche. Phir pata chala uske baachein ho hi nahi sakte. Zindagi phir badal gayi. Lekin bacche ke peeche aisi lagi meri behen, god hi le liya ek beti ko. Zindagi phir badal gayi. Meh keh raha hoon. Vaqt aayega. Aur uska baacchein ke illava koi jawab nahi.

SUMAIRA. Bullshit. Just because your sister, who is only one woman, just had to adopt a child, doesn't mean all women must have a biological clock.

INA. But I don't get it, Sumaira. Why? I've been shutting down shaadi baachein talk for years. And now I'm crying when I see a fake sonogram on TV? It's like... it's like my uterus alarm is ringing. Or rather it's screaming, "have a baby, have a baby now!"

SUMAIRA. Your uterus is an alarm clock now?

INA. I don't know. I'm confused.

SUMAIRA. Well put your uterus on snooze and focus on work. You have plans. Goals? Do you actually want a baby right now?

INA. No. I don't know. Maybe. Not right now. One day.

SHOPKEEPER. Make up your mind ji.

SUMAIRA. Aap se kaun pooch raha hai?

INA. I feel like my body is telling me to do it now.

SUMAIRA. But why? Why can't it wait? For your brain? Or for when it makes any sense at all?

INA. Maybe it can wait. But like truly, Sumaira, every time

I see a baby on the subway, I feel so much and I don't know where these feelings are coming from all of a sudden.

SHOPKEEPER. Dil se.

INA. Nahi dil se nahi hai. It's more physical than that. Uterus se hai.

SUMAIRA. Your uterus does not have thoughts and feelings. Or tear ducts and alarm bells!

INA. No but it clearly has wants and needs.

SHOPKEEPER. Mein uterus ke bade mein nahi jaanta. Lekin dil aur mann ki baat samajh sakta hoon.

INA. Mera mann baccha nahi chahta. Aur mera dil sahi insaan ka intizar karna chahta hai. Lekin yeh rohne ka chakkar pakka uterus se aa raha hai.

SUMAIRA. Can you hear yourself? Your uterus can't make you cry. It can't demand anything of your body. And your heart is pumping blood not feelings.

INA. You don't get it.

SUMAIRA. Aur yeh sahi insaan kaun hai?

INA. Do you want me to say it's you?

SUMAIRA. I don't know. Maybe. But a commitment to me would be a lot better than a baby right now. And if you do want to commit to me, then don't I get a say in all this?

INA. Sumaira, of course you do.

SUMAIRA. Okay well I'm terrified, Ina.

INA. Terrified? Just by the idea?

SUMAIRA. Yes. And maybe one day I won't be, but right now?

INA. We're gonna need more ice cream.

SUMAIRA. I don't want ice cream. And I'd really like to not be having this conversation in the middle of a bodega right now.

INA. Okay. Okay, yeah we should go. Apparently we have a lot to discuss.

SUMAIRA. Apparently?

> (**INA** *and* **SUMAIRA** *start to exit with the ice cream.*)

SHOPKEEPER. Bye ji.

INA. Bye, Uncle.

SUMAIRA. Thank you.

SHOPKEEPER. Koi nahi ji.

> (*The bell over the door jingles as they leave. The* **SHOPKEEPER** *picks up his phone and makes a call.*)

Haan Didi? Kya haal chal?

Bhariya, bhariya.

Sheena kaisi hai?

Arre vah, bahut hoshar hai teri guriya rani.

Zara phone pe la na usse.

Sheena! Hello! Mein Mamu bol raha hoon.

Kaho na Mamu. Mamu.

> (*He listens. She must have said it because he is delighted. He tears up. Pure joy.*)

End of Play

Every Man's Memorial Marked

Maria D. Smith

EVERY MAN'S MEMORIAL MARKED was first produced by Theater Masters via Zoom on May 20, 2021. The performance was directed by Dennis A. Allen II. The production stage manager was Kelly Martindale. The cast was as follows:

JOE DILLARD .... Keith Randolph Smith

SYLVESTER TENNON .... Count Stovall

CHARACTERS

JOE DILLARD – elderly Black man with sharecropper roots, can be played by a young person, but they must embody the age (seventies). Coping with death by disassociating from reality, fighting back at every turn.

SYLVESTER TENNON – also an elderly Black man with sharecropper roots, but with less audacity. Frigid in comparison to his best friend Joe, but having his own sense of wisdom. Also in his seventies but younger than Joe.

(JOE DILLARD sits with his straw hat covering his face. A spotlight sits on him as we ponder if he is dead or alive. After a long silence, JOE snores aggressively. As if his heartbeat is the catalyst for the life of the stage, the spot light expands to reveal the full stage. JOE sits in a raggedy lawn chair, with two similiarly ragged chairs beside him. JOE continues to snore until the sound of a rattley engine is heard approaching. He jolts awake, scrambles his hands around his chest for his glasses. JOE finds his glasses, puts them on, and leans forward in his chair as he squints.)

JOE. Aw hell. Is that Sylvester?

SYLVESTER. *(Offstage.)* Aye yo, Joe!

JOE. Hell, hell, hell! It is.

(JOE, still seated, attempts to collect the empty gin bottles as SYLVESTER TENNON comes in from down stage right. As SYLVESTER is walking, he is waving, until he hears a dog barking as if attacking him at his ankles. SYLVESTER freezes still and puts his hands up, wimpering.)

SYLVESTER. Ah! Joe! Joe! Get ya dog, Joe! Get ya dog!

(JOE is now out of the chair sweeping his area of gin bottles.)

JOE. I ain't Joe no mo', Sylvester!

SYLVESTER. You what?!

JOE. I ain't Joe no mo'.

SYLVESTER. And?! What that got tah do with this damn
dog?! Joe! I swear fo' God, Joe, I'm telling ya! I will
shoot this dog! I will and I won't buy you no new one!

> (**JOE** *is back to sitting in his chair. As he
> sits down, he crosses his legs at the knee and
> takes out a carton of cigarettes, preparing to
> smoke.*)

> (*The dog is still barking and sounds as if
> he's getting closer to* **SYLVESTER**. **JOE** *takes his
> time lighting his cigarette and then taking a
> puff.*)

JOE. Call her bastard, see what happens.

SYLVESTER. Bastard! Get back from me, bastard! Joe, it's
not workin'! Please get this dog, get this dog or I'll kill
it!

JOE. (*Shrugs.*) Kill 'er. That's just another strike for you on
judgement day.

> (*The dog continues to bark until* **JOE** *whistles
> a loud, almost vicious, sound.* **SYLVESTER**,
> now with his eyes squeezed tight, holds for a
> moment, as if waiting to see if his freedom
> is true. A moment passes, before* **SYLVESTER**
> trusts the moment and walks up to sit in the
> chair furthest from* **JOE**.)

> (*A silence.*)

SYLVESTER. Killing a dog ain't never sent nobody to hell.
God believes in self defense. If I shoot ya dog it's self
defense.

JOE. If you wanna argue all that self defense, you move
to Florida. You shoot my dog, you going to hell. White
people say if you kill a dog you go to jail and hell.

SYLVESTER. And if ya dog would have killed me, then

what? It's your dog, your property. My death would be ya fault. It'll be in the paper, too. It'll say, "Local Drunk Joe Dillard Kills Only Friend."

JOE. Well if you don't go to hell for killing my dog, you'll go for lying on me. I ain't had a drink. I ain't had a drink in about...four, five? Four, five weeks ago.

SYLVESTER. I'm not going to nobody's hell, Joe! You've been drankin'. Hell you're drunk now. I know ya.

JOE. You don't know me.

SYLVESTER. I don't know ya?

JOE. Nope.

SYLVESTER. Almost thirty-nine years I known you, and I don't know you? Make it make sense to me Joe.

JOE. For one, you don't even know my damn dog's name.

SYLVESTER. You ain't never had a dog before today!!

> *(A silence. **JOE** takes out one of the near empty bottles and takes a swig.)*

JOE. ...And?

SYLVESTER. Listen, I ain't come over here to play "what's new" with you. Get ya'self together and let's go.

> *(**JOE** starts to laugh and takes another swig. In an absence of words, he hums something melodic.)*

Naw, naw, naw! We ain't doing this today, Joe! Rumor 'round town is it's yo fault. That Ms. Nancy, as good as she was, got caught up in ya ragin' and carryin' on and ended up –

> *(**JOE** stops humming instantly, his light and airy mood sharpening in defense.)*

JOE. Don't even fix yo mouth, ya hear me?! God done took my soul away from me and y'all ignant bastards gonna blame me?! Get off my porch! You heard me, get on!

SYLVESTER. I know what ya doin'. I know exactly what ya doin'. You done got over here and got sloppy drunk 'cause ya hurt. Joe, I understand –

JOE. *(Sucks his teeth.)* Oh, you understand? Thirty something years and that means you understand? Tell me somethin', where's yo woman, huh? She not dead, just down in Grandjunction spending some other nigga's money. Ain't no death. Ain't no heartbreak. You just broke!

SYLVESTER. Joe, I understand –

JOE. How you understand, Sylvester? You don't even listen to me. I *said* I ain't Joe no mo'. And I meant it, damnit. If you wanna know something, know how to listen. So listen to me. You listenin? I ain't goin'!

> (**SYLVESTER** *puts his head in his hands as* **JOE** *extinguishes his cigarette just to light another one.* **SYLVESTER** *gathers himself, and gets up to sit in the chair closest to* **JOE.**)

SYLVESTER. You don't think today is hard for me too? You my best friend. You think I don't hurt fa' ya like I hurt for myself? You tellin' me to listen. You listen! You don't show up for this funeral, then that's it. Sherriff said he gone' come down here and get you *and* me. Said absence is admittin' guilt. That's what you want?

JOE. I told you to leave!

SYLVESTER. Why? So you can cast ya'self more into crazy? Now, I told Ms. Nancy I wasn't gone' do wrong by her, not in life or in death. I'm takin' you to this funeral, if I gotta sick ya own dog on ya to do it.

JOE. *(Chuckles.)* That dog'll have your ass on a leash before you sick it on me.

(*JOE's chuckle explodes into a loud obnoxious laugh. He can barely speak.*)

Aw damn, can you imagine! You on all fours, leash on yo neck – a damn dog, Sly – taking *you* for a walk, commanding *you*. "Walk, talk, Sylvester." "Love, Sylvester." "Don't bite, don't bite! Be nice!"

(*JOE's laughter starts to settle down as he fishes to light another cigarette. They sit in the silence for a minute.*)

SYLVESTER. Joe –

JOE. Now, I done told you I ain't going. You go find Joe, wherever he at, whatever is left of him, and go on.

SYLVESTER. That's what I'm doing! I came to get ya, so if you'd just get in the truck –

JOE. That piece of junk? Ha!

SYLVESTER. What I do to you, huh? I'm here 'cause I'm ya friend, tryin' to help. Hell! Tryin' to save ya life, and you can't even say "thank you"? Huh? If sheriff didn't have my ass on the line too, I'd leave you here.

(*JOE gets out of his chair and walks toward the pile of old toys. He picks up a large toy truck and opens the trunk of it to retrieve a bottle of gin.*)

(*He opens it and guzzles it as* SYLVESTER *watches him, waiting.* JOE *finishes his gulp and sits back down and lights another cigarette. His gin now in his front shirt pocket.*)

JOE. (*To himself.*) You know, the only person who's ever known the depths of my soul is getting put in the ground today. I ain't ever been worth nothin' without that woman and now that she gone, I don't know who

I am, what I am... So gone' head. Tell sheriff I'm here. I'm out of time anyway.

  (A silence.)

SYLVESTER. I'm not saying I understand, but I'll say what I feel, and I feel like you're allowed to live. I feel, well, I feel that if Joe is dead, well, that's OK.

JOE. It's gone' have to be.

SYLVESTER. You right.

JOE. I know I am. You just agreeing with me to mock me, but I know I'm right. When I ain't Joe, I'm right.

   (**JOE** *takes the gin from his shirt pocket and takes a swig.* **SYLVESTER** *watches him and puts his hand out to take a turn.* **JOE** *hesitates at first, and then gives up the bottle.)*

SYLVESTER. I ain't mockin' you. I swear for God I ain't. You right. Ain't no woman ever saw enough in me to take me for life. Some of 'em gave me kids, but they ain't never ever gave me them.

JOE. Just 'cause I married her don't mean I had her.

   (**SYLVESTER** *hands the bottle back to* **JOE**. *They now get in a rhythmic rotation of sharing the bottle.)*

SYLVESTER. No?

JOE. Naw. I mean, I had her in doses, but I never had *her.* Some days I knew exactly who she was, others, it was like I woke up with a stranger. But maybe that was more Joe than her. Now he's out there just trying to get the last notes of her voice in his ear... But that's on Joe. That's why I ain't him.

SYLVESTER. I never saw it that way.

JOE. Seein' and existin' are two different things. You exist in shame, can't see it though. Play it off as power if you need to. Hell, as a man, you got to…

SYLVESTER. So when do we bury Joe?

JOE. We don't.

SYLVESTER. Now that ain't right. Every man deserves a memorial, some flowers on they grave at least.

JOE. Joe don't.

SYLVESTER. It might not be my place to say, but I don't agree. If Joe is dead, we should bury him. Let him know that we saw him trying, at least.

JOE. You give memorials to people who tried and just ran out of time. Joe ain't never try 'cause her love was always a given. You don't give flowers to that. You let it whither up and rot in all that regret he got. Let him sit in it and drown.

(*A silence.*)

SYLVESTER. Sheriff said he can't hold you if the autopsy come back clean. I told 'em it would, but he said he gotta do his job and'll take me down with ya.

Just waiting to use my past against me. I told 'em she died in her sleep, but he don't listen. Just waving that badge around. Said he'd heard too many things for too long. And the miscarriage from years back don't help, the way she got rushed in. Said she wouldn't let 'em pin nothin' on you before, but now –

JOE. Yeah.

(**JOE** *stops the rhythmic rotation of the bottle and snatches it away from* **SYLVESTER** *mid-sip.*)

(*A silence.*)

SYLVESTER. Can I ask you?

JOE. Ask me what?

SYLVESTER. That day you called me up to drive her to the hospital? I ain't ask no questions but –

> *(A silence. It takes a while for anything to come out.)*

JOE. She found out I had a kid across town. I don't think I've evah seen anybody's eyes hurt so bad. And what do I say, ya know? She's mad, so I'm mad. Naw, I'm mad, but she *hurt*. And I just – I couldn't even look at her.

SYLVESTER. Oh.

JOE. She was 'bout out the door. I call myself pulling her back in. Should've let her go 'cause next thing I know, she ain't OK. I dunno what happened but she wasn't OK. So I called you.

SYLVESTER. And she stayed?

JOE. Said God told her to forgive.

> *(**SYLVESTER** and **JOE** sit in silence, avoiding each other's eyes.)*

> *(**SYLVESTER** goes to exit from the stage right he entered from. **JOE** finishes off the rest of the bottle of gin before getting up from his own chair. Seeing **JOE** get up as he passes by him, **SYLVESTER** stops and turns around.)*

If we buried Joe, what would you say 'bout him?

SYLVESTER. If I had to say anything, I'd say he was big. Bigger than where he come from, bigger than what he been through, just big. He'd tell you who he was before he showed you, but once he showed you, you couldn't unsee it. But that was Joe, ya know? A man of his own. *(Chuckles.)* I tell you what, he was a sore loser! I ain't never seen nothing like it. I can never forget him. Hell, I loved 'em, but I – I couldn't hold his burdens for 'em.

(JOE turns his back on SYLVESTER as he contemplates. SYLVESTER takes a few steps to JOE as if to reach out and say something. Before he can commit to getting JOE's attention SYLVESTER pivots away and exits off stage. As soon as JOE goes to turn around to respond to SYLVESTER, he is greeted by the reving of the truck engine and the sound of it driving away. The dog barks. JOE stands up and picks up one of the newspapers, flips it open, acts as if he's reading.)

JOE. On today, at this time, Joe died. He was born in the sticks, worked in the bricks, and didn't take nobody's shit. *(Chuckles.)* Naw, Joe was scared. He ain't take no shit 'cause he was shittin' himself. He say he woke up ready to fight the world. The world hit 'em, he hit 'em back, blow for blow. Heavy weight champ of his world by far, but even the champ takes a dive sometimes. But Joe fought so much, sometimes he fought the wrong thing. Joe had somethin', a woman, that gave him life, but he even fought her. Just figured if he was fightin' than she should be too. Said she was there to fight, but Joe ain't believe her. He let her wear herself out. But when she died, she took all Joe's fight with 'er. And now he dead, too. He was loved, but ain't know how to love. Alive, but ain't live a life worth remembering. So now, he just dead. Dead and regrettin'...

(JOE folds the newspaper under his arm and proceeds to pour out his gin.)

End